ADAPTED BY SCOTT PETERSON

Disney PRESS

New York

Artwork for *Lion King* by Sparky Moore, Jo Meugniot, Chagnaud/Yot
Artwork for *Pinocchio* by Hank Porter, Bob Grant, Gianfranco Grieco, Jean-Jacques Changnaud
Artwork for *Bambi* by Comicup Studio, Mario Cortes, Jean-Jaques Changnaud

For information address Disney Press, 114 Fifth Avenue, New York, NY 10011-5690.
Bambi from the story by Felix Salten
Printed in Singapore
First Edition
1 3 5 7 9 10 8 6 4 2
Library of Congress Catalog Card Number on file.

ISBN 0-7868-3517-6

For more Disney Press fun, visit www.disneybooks.com

CONTENTS

THE AFRICAN SAVANNA. HOME TO THE ANTELOPE, THE WILDEBEEST, ZEBRA, COUNTLESS BIRDS AND MANY OTHER ANIMALS. AND ALSO HOME, OF COURSE, TO THE KING OF THE BEASTS—THE MIGHTY LION!

ANOTHER NEW DAWN IN AFRICA . . .

. . . ANOTHER DAY TO SEE, TO HEAR, TO SMELL, TO DO . . .

. . . TO LIVE!

LIFE HOLDS SO MUCH PROMISE, AND TIME SEEMS SO SHORT . . .

BUT EVEN AS THE GREAT CIRCLE OF THE SUN BEGINS ITS JOURNEY ACROSS THE ENDLESS SKIES AGAIN . . .

TODAY, A NEW LIFE BEGINS ITS *OWN* JOURNEY . . .

. . . THE JOURNEY CALLED LIVING . . .

. . . AND A SEARCH FOR A PLACE IN THE GREAT CIRCLE OF LIFE!

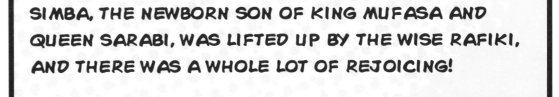

SIMBA, THE NEWBORN SON OF KING MUFASA AND QUEEN SARABI, WAS LIFTED UP BY THE WISE RAFIKI, AND THERE WAS A WHOLE LOT OF REJOICING!

BUT NOT *EVERYONE* WAS OVERJOYED ABOUT THE ARRIVAL OF THE NEW PRINCE. IN FACT, THE KING'S OWN BROTHER WAS NOT HAPPY AT *ALL*.

KING MUFASA DIDN'T TAKE KINDLY TO THREATS FROM ANYONE. WHILE HE LOVED HIS BROTHER, HE JUST DIDN'T KNOW WHAT TO DO ABOUT HIS BAD ATTITUDE. HE KNEW HE'D NEED TO KEEP AN EYE ON HIM. IN THE MEANTIME, MUFASA HAD THINGS HE NEEDED TO TEACH SIMBA.

ONE DAY THE SUN WILL SET ON MY TIME HERE, AND RISE WITH YOU AS THE NEW KING.

AND ALL THIS WILL BE *MINE*?

EVERYTHING.

WHAT ABOUT THAT SHADOWY PLACE?

THAT'S BEYOND OUR BORDERS. YOU MUST NEVER GO THERE, SIMBA.

BUT I THOUGHT A KING COULD DO WHATEVER HE WANTS!

WHILE MUFASA WAS CHECKING OUT THE HYENA SITUATION, SIMBA VISITED HIS UNCLE SCAR TO TELL HIM ALL ABOUT WHAT MUFASA HAD SAID. SIMBA EVEN TOLD SCAR ABOUT THE SHADOWY PLACE.

YOUR FATHER IS RIGHT. ONLY THE BRAVEST LIONS GO TO THE SHADOWY PLACE.

WELL, *I'M* BRAVE—WHAT'S OUT THERE?

SIMBA . . . AN ELEPHANT GRAVEYARD IS NO PLACE FOR . . .

AN ELEPHANT *WHAT*!?

SIMBA WAS SUDDENLY VERY CURIOUS.

SOON AFTER, ON PRIDE ROCK . . .

HEY, NALA!

HI, SIMBA

COME ON! I JUST HEARD ABOUT THIS *GREAT PLACE!*

I'M KINDA IN THE MIDDLE OF A *BATH.*

BUT IT'S REALLY COOL! IT'S AROUND THE *WATERHOLE* . . .

THE WATERHOLE?! WHAT'S SO GREAT ABOUT THE *WATERHOLE?*

I'LL SHOW YOU WHEN WE GET THERE!

OOOOOH . . .

SIMBA AND NALA WERE ALLOWED TO GO TO THE WATERHOLE—BUT ONLY IF THEY BROUGHT ZAZU ALONG WITH THEM.

THE TWO CUBS FOUND THEMSELVES IN A VERY UNFAMILIAR PLACE.

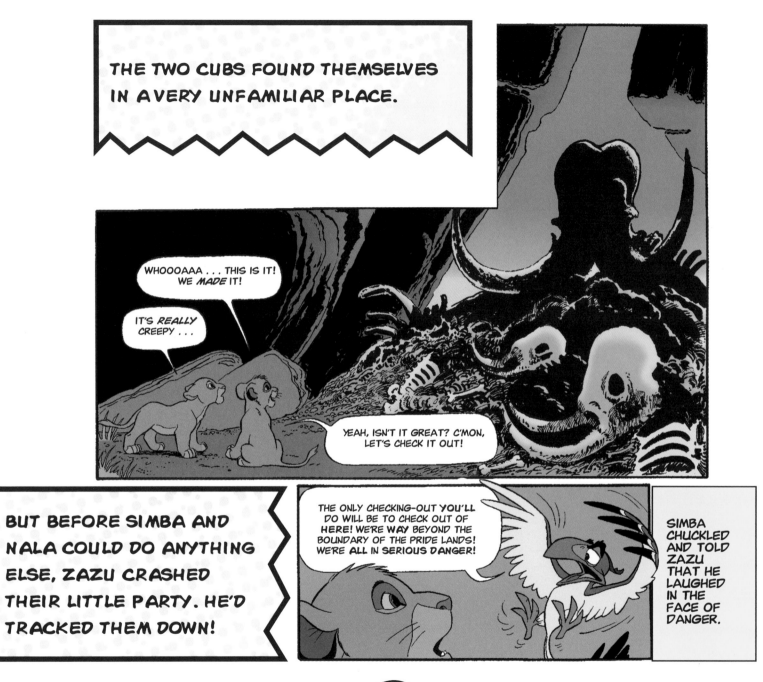

WHOOOAAA . . . THIS IS IT! WE *MADE* IT!

IT'S *REALLY* CREEPY . . .

YEAH, ISN'T IT GREAT? C'MON, LET'S CHECK IT OUT!

BUT BEFORE SIMBA AND NALA COULD DO ANYTHING ELSE, ZAZU CRASHED THEIR LITTLE PARTY. HE'D TRACKED THEM DOWN!

THE ONLY CHECKING-OUT YOU'LL DO WILL BE TO CHECK OUT OF HERE! WE'RE WAY BEYOND THE BOUNDARY OF THE PRIDE LANDS! WE'RE ALL IN SERIOUS DANGER!

SIMBA CHUCKLED AND TOLD ZAZU THAT HE LAUGHED IN THE FACE OF DANGER.

...THEN, THE HYENAS SHOWED UP!

HEE HEE HEE

WELL, WELL, WHAT HAVE WE GOT HERE?

I DO BELIEVE WE'VE HIT THE JACKPOT!

SO YOU'RE—

THE FUTURE KING!

ZAZU TRIED TO ESCAPE WITH HIS FRIENDS!
BUT THE HYENAS HAD OTHER PLANS . . .

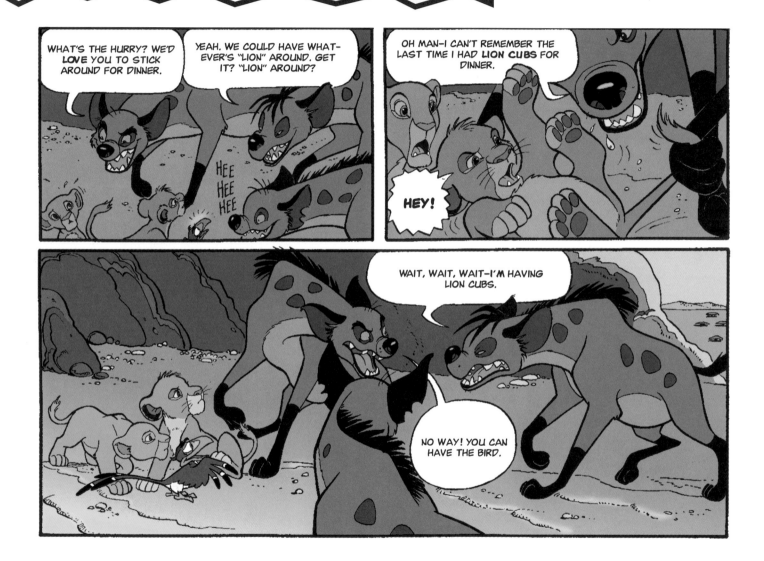

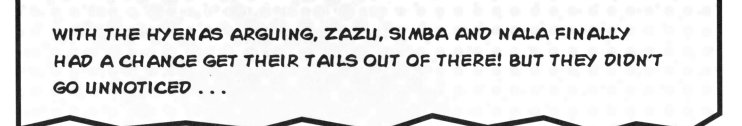

WITH THE HYENAS ARGUING, ZAZU, SIMBA AND NALA FINALLY HAD A CHANCE GET THEIR TAILS OUT OF THERE! BUT THEY DIDN'T GO UNNOTICED . . .

HEY, DID WE ORDER THIS DINNER TO GO?

NO—WHY?

'CAUSE THERE IT GOES!

GET 'EM!

HURRY, NALA!

I AM!

BUT WHILE HE WAS RUNNING, SIMBA NOTICED THAT ZAZU WAS GONE. SIMBA MAY HAVE WANTED TO DITCH THE BIRD BEFORE, BUT NOW HE WISHED HIS FRIEND WAS WITH HIM. ESPECIALLY SINCE HE AND NALA WERE ABOUT TO DISCOVER JUST HOW FRIGHTENING THIS UNFAMILIAR PLACE REALLY WAS! THE CUBS TRIPPED AND FELL . . .

NEEDLESS TO SAY, THE KING WAS **NOT** HAPPY WITH THE DAY'S EVENTS. IT WAS TIME HE HAD ANOTHER FATHER-SON CHAT WITH HIS CUB.

SIMBA, I'M *VERY* DISAPPOINTED IN YOU.

I KNOW.

YOU COULD HAVE BEEN *KILLED.* YOU DISOBEYED ME—AND WHAT'S WORSE, YOU PUT *NALA* IN DANGER!

BUT I WAS JUST TRYING TO BE BRAVE, LIKE *YOU.*

I'M ONLY BRAVE WHEN I *HAVE* TO BE, SIMBA.

BEING BRAVE DOESN'T MEAN YOU GO *LOOK-ING* FOR TROUBLE.

BUT *YOU'RE* NOT SCARED OF *ANYTHING!*

I WAS TODAY.

YOU *WERE?*

SIMBA AND MUFASA WRESTLED PLAYFULLY. IT WAS CLEAR THAT ALL WAS FORGIVEN.

MUFASA BECAME SERIOUS, AND THEN HE TURNED TO HIS SON.

SIMBA, LET ME TELL YOU SOMETHING MY FATHER TOLD ME. LOOK AT THE STARS. THE GREAT KINGS OF THE PAST STARE DOWN ON US FROM THOSE STARS.

REALLY?

YES. SO WHENEVER YOU FEEL ALONE, JUST REMEMBER THAT THOSE KINGS WILL ALWAYS BE THERE TO GUIDE YOU.

AND SO WILL I.

AS USUAL, SIMBA'S DAD MADE HIM FEEL A LOT BETTER.

BUT ELSE-WHERE, AT THAT VERY MOMENT, EVIL WAS STILL BREWING.

I GIVE MERE *CUBS* TO YOU, AND YOU FOOLS CAN'T EVEN DISPOSE OF THEM.

THIS IS THE CHANCE OF A LIFETIME. STICK WITH ME AND YOU'LL NEVER GO HUNGRY AGAIN. BUT YOU MUST BE PREPARED!

YEAH, WE'LL BE PREPARED! UH . . . FOR WHAT?

FOR THE *DEATH* OF THE *KING*.

WE'RE GOING TO KILL HIM—AND SIMBA TOO. THEN *I* WILL BE KING!

LONG LIVE THE KING!

HEE HEE HEE HEE HEE

IT WASN'T LONG BEFORE SCAR BEGAN TO PUT HIS PLAN INTO ACTION. HE BROUGHT SIMBA TO A ROCK IN A GORGE.

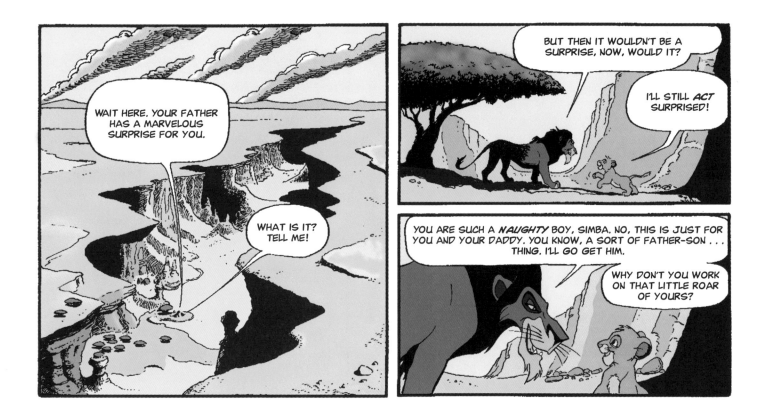

WAIT HERE. YOUR FATHER HAS A MARVELOUS SURPRISE FOR YOU.

WHAT IS IT? TELL ME!

BUT THEN IT WOULDN'T BE A SURPRISE, NOW, WOULD IT?

I'LL STILL *ACT* SURPRISED!

YOU ARE SUCH A *NAUGHTY* BOY, SIMBA. NO, THIS IS JUST FOR YOU AND YOUR DADDY. YOU KNOW, A SORT OF FATHER-SON . . . THING. I'LL GO GET HIM.

WHY DON'T YOU WORK ON THAT LITTLE ROAR OF YOURS?

'LITTLE ROAR!'
PUH!

WHILE SIMBA PRACTICED HIS ROARING IN THE GORGE, HIS UNCLE SKULKED AWAY, PROUD OF HIMSELF FOR BEING SO SLICK AND SNEAKY. SCAR GAVE THE HYENAS A SIGNAL AND THE VERY NEXT MOMENT THE GROUND BELOW SIMBA'S PAWS BEGAN TO SHAKE VIOLENTLY. SIMBA HAD NO CLUE WHAT WAS HAPPENING.

HUH?

GASP!

THEN SIMBA TURNED TO SEE THAT THE WILDEBEESTS WERE ON THE MOVE! AND, THEY WERE THUNDERING TOWARD *HIM*!

RRRRUMBLE! RRRRUMBLE!

THE GREAT HERD MOVED LIKE A FLOOD . . .

. . . CRUSHING EVERYTHING IN ITS PATH.

BUT THERE WAS A *REASON* THE WILDE-BEESTS WERE ALL RUNNING.

THE HYENAS, AT SCAR'S COMMAND, WERE NIPPING AT THE WILDEBEESTS' HEELS TO SCARE THEM! THEY WERE CAUSING THE STAMPEDE!

AND CLOSE BY . . .

LOOK, SIRE—THE HERD IS ON THE MOVE!

THAT'S ODD . . .

THEN, SCAR SHOWED UP.

MUFASA—*QUICK*! STAMPEDE! IN THE GORGE! *SIMBA'S* DOWN THERE!

SIMBA?!

HELP!!!

...BUT THE KING HIMSELF WAS NOT SO LUCKY, AND HE BEGAN TO PANIC AS HE SLIPPED BACK INTO THE GORGE!

MUFASA CALLED OUT TO HIS BROTHER SCAR, WHO STOOD SAFELY ON THE LEDGE ABOVE HIM.

SCAR! PLEASE! HELP ME, MY BROTHER!

BUT INSTEAD OF HELPING HIM OUT, SCAR DUG HIS CLAWS INTO MUFASA SO THAT HE COULDN'T HOLD ON ANY LONGER. THE PROUD KING FELL INTO THE GORGE AND WAS CAUGHT IN THE STAMPEDE. SCAR WAS VICTORIOUS.

LONG LIVE THE KING!

SIMBA WATCHED IN SHOCK AS HIS FATHER FELL. HE RAN TO HIM WHEN THE STAMPEDE PASSED.

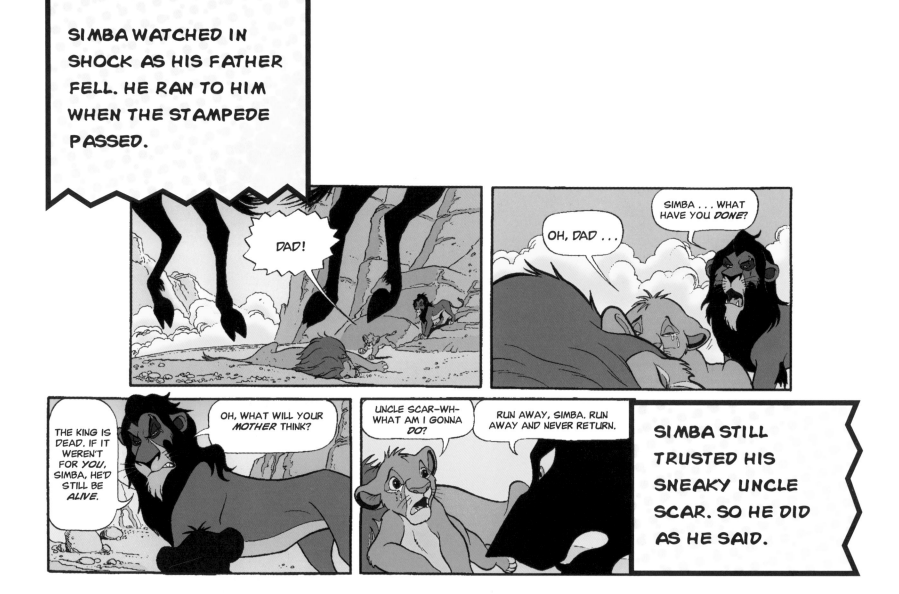

WHILE SIMBA WAS WANDERING AROUND THE DESERT, ALONE, SCARED, AND LOOKING FOR WATER, SCAR CLIMBED TO THE TOP OF PRIDE ROCK.

TIMON TOLD PUMBAA THAT LIONS ATE GUYS LIKE THEM. IT WASN'T A GOOD IDEA TO BE HANGING AROUND ONE. BUT PUMBAA WANTED TO TAKE SIMBA ALONG WITH THEM, EVEN IF, *IN GENERAL*, LIONS WERE DANGEROUS.

AND SO THE SMALL BAND OF MISFITS MOVED ON, GROWING CLOSER, AND BECOMING FRIENDS. TIME PASSED.

AND SIMBA GREW INTO A BIG, PROUD LION.

EVER WONDER WHAT THOSE SPARKLY DOTS ARE UP THERE?

SOMEONE ONCE TOLD ME THE GREAT KINGS OF THE PAST ARE UP THERE, WATCHING OVER US.

YA MEAN A BUNCH OF ROYAL DEAD GUYS ARE LOOKIN' AT US? THAT'S THE CRAZIEST THING I EVER HEARD.

YEAH. PRETTY DUMB, HUH?

SIMBA!
IT IS TIME . . . .

MEANWHILE, BACK IN THE JUNGLE, A NEW DAY HAD DAWNED AND IT WAS BUSINESS AS USUAL. BUT SOMETHING VERY UNEXPECTED WAS ABOUT TO HAPPEN!

YIKES!

ROAR!

SQUEEEAL!

PUMBAA RAN AS FAST AS HE COULD.

ROAR!

BUT HE GOT STUCK IN A TREE! SIMBA WASN'T ABOUT TO LET SOME WILD ANIMAL HAVE HIS FRIEND FOR LUNCH.

BUT AS SIMBA PREPARED TO STRIKE, HE REALIZED THAT THE ANIMAL WHO HAD ATTACKED PUMBAA WAS NOT SO UNFAMILIAR AT ALL! IT WAS NALA!

NALA! IT'S ME—SIMBA!

SIMBA?

IT'S *GREAT* TO SEE YOU, NALA!

SIMBA! IT'S GREAT TO SEE YOU, TOO! BUT WHAT ARE YOU *DOING* HERE?

I LIVE HERE!

NALA WAS REALLY EXCITED TO SEE HER OLD PAL. BUT SHE WAS ALSO *CONFUSED*!

BUT SIMBA—EVERYONE THINKS YOU'RE *DEAD*. SCAR TOLD US ABOUT THE STAMPEDE.

WHAT . . . WHAT ELSE DID HE TELL YOU?

WHAT ELSE *MATTERS*? YOU'RE ALIVE! AND THAT MEANS—

YOU'RE THE KING.

NO, I'M NOT THE KING. MAYBE I WAS *GOING* TO BE, BUT THAT WAS A LONG TIME AGO. THINGS . . . CHANGE.

WHOA! YOU'RE THE *KING*? AND YOU NEVER *TOLD* US?!

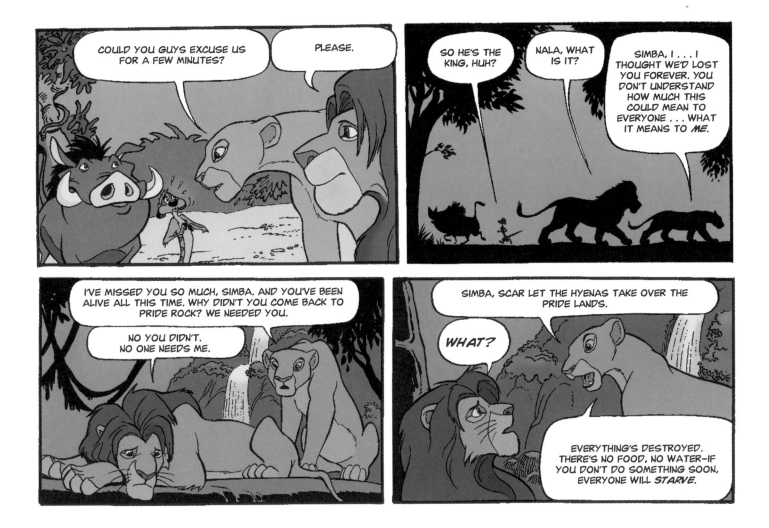

BUT SIMBA WAS WAY TOO SCARED TO RETURN. HE WAS AFRAID TO FACE HIS PAST.

SIMBA, IT'S YOUR BIRTHRIGHT—YOUR RESPONSIBILITY! DOESN'T THE PRIDE MEAN ANYTHING TO YOU?

YOU LEFT!

TO FIND *HELP*—AND I FOUND *YOU*. BUT YOU'RE NOT THE SIMBA I REMEMBER.

YOU'RE RIGHT. I'M NOT. *NOW* ARE YOU SATISFIED?

NO. JUST *DISAPPOINTED*.

YOU KNOW, YOU SOUND LIKE MY FATHER.

GOOD. AT LEAST ONE OF US DOES.

RAFIKI SAID THAT MUFASA LIVED INSIDE SIMBA. AND THEN SOMETHING AMAZING HAPPENED. IT WAS AS IF MUFASA WAS RIGHT THERE TALKING TO SIMBA!

SIMBA STARTED TO THINK ABOUT THE PAST AND ALL THE THINGS THAT HAD HAPPENED TO HIM.

MY FATHER'S DEATH . . . WAS . . . *MY* FAULT.

OW!

WHAT WAS *THAT* FOR?

IT DOESN'T MATTER. IT'S IN THE PAST.

YEAH, BUT IT STILL *HURTS.*

OH, YES . . .

. . . THE PAST CAN HURT. BUT YOU CAN EITHER *RUN* FROM IT . . . OR YOU CAN *LEARN* FROM IT.

MAYBE IT'S TIME TO STOP RUNNING.

SIMBA KNEW RAFIKI WAS RIGHT, AND SO HE RETURNED TO HIS HOME—HE RETURNED TO THE PRIDE LANDS!

WHEN SIMBA ARRIVED AT HIS KINGDOM, HE HARDLY RECOGNIZED IT. AND THEN HE DISCOVERED HE WASN'T ALONE!

YOU FORGOT TO SAY GOOD-BYE, SIMBA.

NALA! I . . . I FORGOT TO SAY A *LOT* OF THINGS. I THOUGHT I'D NEVER SEE YOU AGAIN, AFTER—

SIMBA—WHATEVER I SAID, IT WAS BECAUSE I *CARE* ABOUT YOU.

NO—YOU WERE RIGHT.

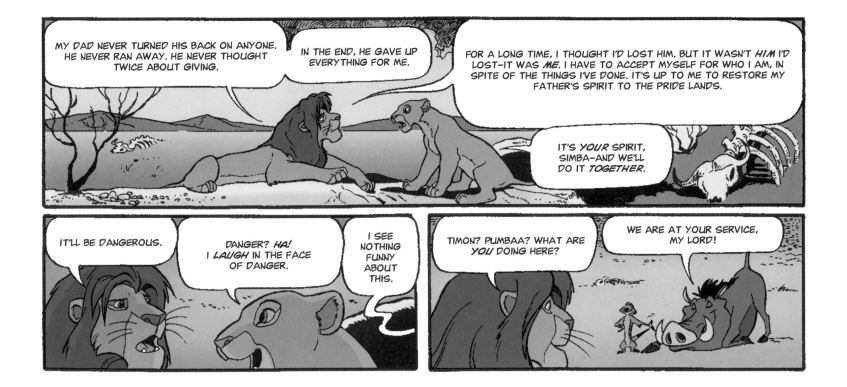

TIMON TOOK A QUICK LOOK AT THE BARREN LAND AND
WONDERED WHY *ANYONE* WOULD FIGHT FOR IT.

WE'RE GONNA FIGHT YOUR UNCLE . . . FOR *THIS*?

TALK ABOUT YOUR FIXER-UPPER!

YES, TIMON. THIS IS MY HOME.

WELL, SIMBA, IF IT'S IMPORTANT TO YOU, WE'RE WITH YOU TO THE END!

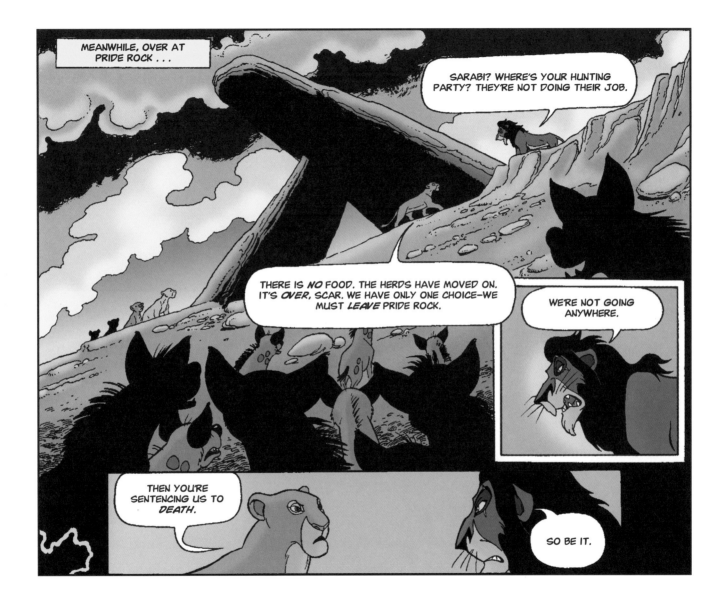

SARABI WAS GETTING VERY ANGRY, AND SHE WASN'T AFRAID TO SHOW IT!

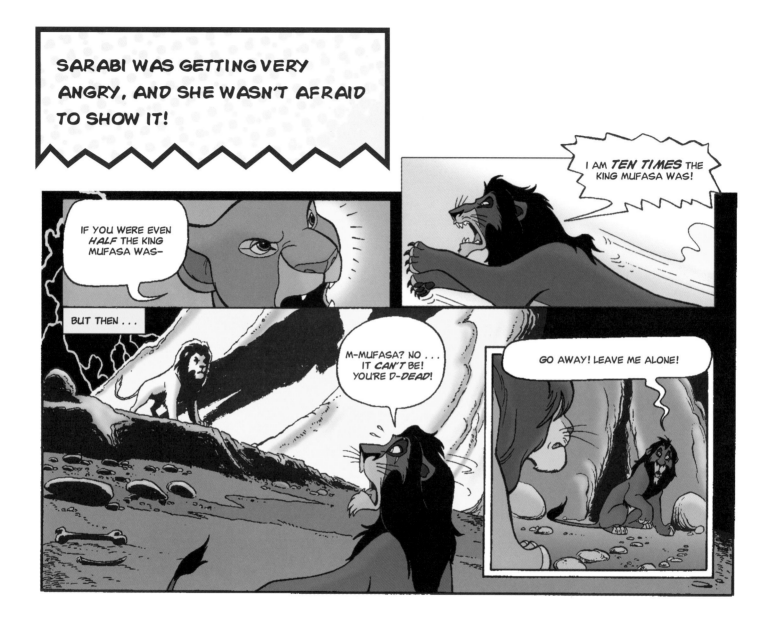

IF YOU WERE EVEN *HALF* THE KING MUFASA WAS—

I AM *TEN TIMES* THE KING MUFASA WAS!

BUT THEN . . .

M-MUFASA? NO . . . IT *CAN'T* BE! YOU'RE D-*DEAD*!

GO AWAY! LEAVE ME ALONE!

SIMBA WAS READY TO CONFRONT SCAR, BUT HE WAS NOT GOING TO PRETEND HE WAS SOMEONE HE WASN'T.

MUFASA?

NO, IT'S ME, SIMBA. I'M HOME.

IT'S YOUR CHOICE, SCAR—STEP DOWN OR FIGHT.

OH, PLEASE—MUST THIS ALL END IN VIOLENCE?

I'D JUST *HATE* TO BE RESPONSIBLE FOR THE DEATH OF A FAMILY MEMBER—WOULDN'T YOU?

THAT'S NOT GOING TO WORK, SCAR. I'VE PUT IT BEHIND ME.

AH, BUT WHAT ABOUT YOUR SUBJECTS? HAVE *THEY* FORGIVEN YOU?

WHAT IS HE TALKING ABOUT?

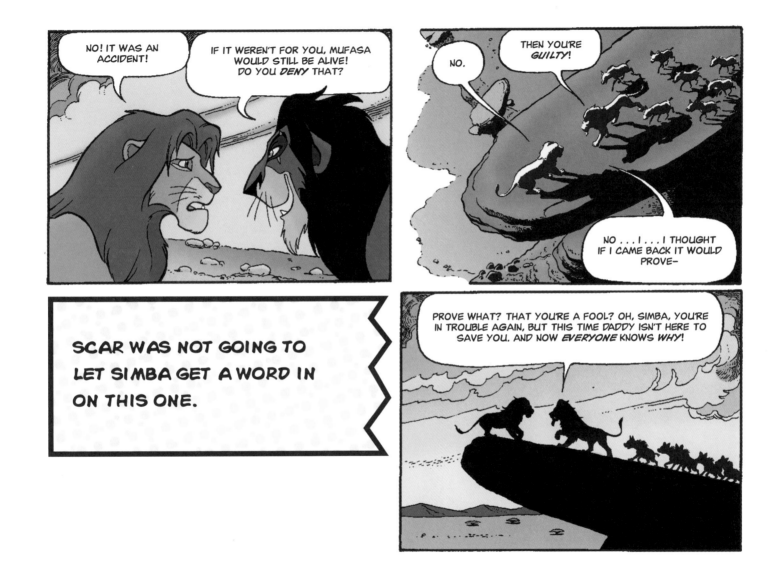

SCAR WAS NOT GOING TO LET SIMBA GET A WORD IN ON THIS ONE.

AS SCAR ADVANCED ON HIM, SIMBA SLIPPED AND BEGAN TO SLIDE OFF THE CLIFF!

RRAAAAA!!!

NOW *THIS* LOOKS FAMILIAR. WHERE HAVE I SEEN THIS BEFORE? LET ME *THINK* . . .

OH, YES, *I* REMEMBER. THAT'S *JUST* THE WAY YOUR *FATHER* LOOKED . . . BEFORE *HE* DIED.

AND HERE'S *MY* LITTLE SECRET . . .

. . . *I* KILLED MUFASA!

SCAR LEAPED UP TO ATTACK SIMBA. BUT SIMBA WAS READY.
SCAR FELL FROM THE CLIFF. HIS EVIL WAYS HAD PROVED TO BE HIS UNDOING.

THE REIGN OF THE FALSE KING WAS FINALLY OVER! PROSPERITY RETURNED TO THE PRIDE LANDS. AND THE GREAT CIRCLE OF LIFE CONTINUED . . .

ANOTHER NEW DAWN IN AFRICA.

LIFE HOLDS SO MUCH PROMISE, AND TIME SEEMS SO SHORT.

ON THIS DAY, ANOTHER NEW LIFE BEGINS ITS JOURNEY, THE JOURNEY CALLED LIVING . . .

. . . AND ANOTHER SEARCH FOR A PLACE IN THE GREAT CIRCLE OF LIFE!

THE END

Pinocchio

HI THERE! MY NAME'S CRICKET—JIMINY CRICKET. I BET YOU DON'T BELIEVE THAT WISHES CAN COME TRUE.

WELL, I CAN'T BLAME YOU! I DIDN'T EITHER. THEN, ONE NIGHT—A LONG TIME AGO . . .

". . . MY TRAVELS TOOK ME TO A COZY LITTLE VILLAGE. IT WAS A BEAUTIFUL NIGHT. THE STARS WERE SHINING LIKE DIAMONDS. IT WAS AS PRETTY AS A PICTURE!"

THE VILLAGE WAS SO QUIET, YOU COULD HARDLY HEAR . . . AHEM . . . A CRICKET CHIRPING. AND AS JIMINY WANDERED ALONG THE WINDING STREETS, THERE WASN'T A SOUL TO BE SEEN.

THE ONLY SIGN OF LIFE WAS THE LIGHTED WINDOW IN THE SHOP OF A WOODCARVER NAMED GEPPETTO. JIMINY HOPPED OVER AND LOOKED INSIDE.

A FLAMING LOG CRACKLED IN THE FIREPLACE. IT WOULD BE A SHAME TO LET A FIRE LIKE THAT GO TO WASTE, SO JIMINY SNEAKED IN.

INSIDE, THE HOUSE WAS TOASTY WARM. AND IT WAS SOMETHING ELSE TOO—AN AMAZING FACTORY OF WOODEN INVENTIONS!

THERE WERE CLOCKS AND TOYS OF NEARLY EVERY SHAPE AND SIZE. JIMINY HAD NEVER SEEN ANY-THING LIKE IT!

THEN SOMETHING CAUGHT JIMINY'S EYE—A PUPPET! YOU KNOW, ONE OF THOSE MARIONETTE THINGS—ALL STRINGS AND JOINTS!

JIMINY WAS FASCINATED BY THE CUTE LITTLE FELLOW. BUT NOT SO MUCH SO THAT HE DIDN'T RUN FOR COVER WHEN HE HEARD SOMEONE COMING DOWNSTAIRS!

THE HOUSE SEEMED SAFE ENOUGH, BUT A CRICKET CAN'T BE TOO CAREFUL!

SO, WITHOUT A SECOND TO LOSE, JIMINY DECIDED TO DISAPPEAR!

AS THE NOISE GOT CLOSER, JIMINY SAW WHO WAS HEADING HIS WAY. IT WAS GEPPETTO, THE MAN WHO OWNED THE HOUSE—AND WHO HAD MADE THAT PUPPET!

ONE LAST TOUCH OF PAINT, AND HE WILL ALMOST BE LIKE A REAL BOY, WON'T HE, FIGARO?

AND DON'T *YOU* AGREE, CLEO, MY LITTLE FISH?

AND NOW, I HAVE JUST THE NAME FOR YOU . . .

PINOCCHIO!

GEPPETTO TURNED ON A MUSIC BOX AND PICKED UP PINOCCHIO.

AH, PINOCCHIO! COME ON, WE'LL TRY YOU OUT!

GEPPETTO DANCED AROUND WITH HIS PUPPET UNTIL HE FELT TIRED. HE SAID GOODNIGHT TO PINOCCHIO AND WENT TO BED.

YOU KNOW, FIGARO, I'VE ALWAYS DREAMED OF HAVING A SON. AND IF I DID, I HOPE HE'D BE JUST LIKE PINOCCHIO.

LOOK, FIGARO! A SHOOTING STAR! A *WISHING* STAR! I WISH MY PINOCCHIO MIGHT BE A REAL BOY . . . .

JIMINY THOUGHT GEPPETTO'S WISH WAS VERY NICE, BUT NOT VERY PRACTICAL. THEN THE CRICKET DECIDED TO TURN IN FOR THE NIGHT HIMSELF.

NOW, JIMINY WASN'T BORN YESTERDAY, SO HE KNEW THAT HAVING A FAIRY SUDDENLY APPEAR MIGHT JUST MEAN THAT GEPPETTO WOULD BE GRANTED HIS WISH AFTER ALL!

LITTLE PUPPET, MADE OF PINE . . .

. . . AWAKE!

THE GIFT OF LIFE IS THINE!

I CAN MOVE! I CAN TALK!

I CAN WALK!!!

WOW. IT'S AMAZING WHAT THEY CAN DO THESE DAYS.

THEN THE BLUE FAIRY TURNED TO JIMINY. NEEDLESS TO SAY, TALKING TO A FAIRY IS NOT EXACTLY EASY . . .

WOULD YOU LIKE TO BE PINOCCHIO'S CONSCIENCE?

WELL—UH—WELL—I—UH UHUH!

VERY WELL, I NAME YOU PINOCCHIO'S CONSCIENCE—LORD HIGH KEEPER OF THE KNOWLEDGE OF RIGHT AND WRONG.

OOH, AND A NEW SUIT TO GO WITH IT! THANK YOU, MA'AM!

AND THEN, AS SUDDENLY AS THE BLUE FAIRY ARRIVED, SHE WAS GONE!

WOW!

THAT WAS SOMETHING!

JIMINY'S FIRST LESSON IN BEING A CONSCIENCE: IT'S NOT JUST **WHAT** YOU SAY, BUT ALSO **WHEN** YOU SAY IT!

A WOODEN BOY LANDING ON A WOODEN FLOOR MAKES A PRETTY LOUD BANG, AND THE SOUND WOKE UP GEPPETTO.

WHAT'S ALL THAT NOISE? WHO'S THERE?

IT'S ME!

THERE'S SOMEBODY IN HERE—

BE CAREFUL, FIGARO . . .

OH, PINOCCHIO. HOW DID YOU GET DOWN HERE?

I FELL DOWN!

WHEN GEPPETTO HEARD PINOCCHIO SPEAK, HE THOUGHT HE WAS DREAMING. BUT PINOCCHIO KEPT TALKING AND GEPPETTO REALIZED THIS WAS NO FANTASY!

A REAL BOY!

IT'S MY WISH! IT'S COME TRUE!

THIS IS THE BEST DAY OF MY ENTIRE LIFE! WE'RE GOING TO BE SO HAPPY TOGETHER!

WE SURE WILL!

THE NEXT MORNING, GEPPETTO GOT PINOCCHIO READY FOR HIS FIRST DAY OF SCHOOL— HIS FIRST DAY IN THE **WORLD**, ACTUALLY!

OH LOOK, FATHER—WHAT ARE THOSE?

THOSE ARE GIRLS AND BOYS.

REAL BOYS?

YES, INDEED, PINOCCHIO—YOUR NEW SCHOOL-MATES! YOU'LL HAVE SUCH FUN WITH THEM!

NOW OFF YOU GO. AND REMEMBER TO BE GOOD!

YES, FATHER—I WILL!

GEPPETTO MAY HAVE BEEN VERY HAPPY. BUT JIMINY WAS ABOUT TO LEARN THAT HE HAD HIS WORK CUT OUT FOR HIM, AS TWO SHADY CHARACTERS CALLED HONEST JOHN AND GIDEON—GIDDY FOR SHORT—CAME TO TOWN.

GIDDY, MY FRIEND, IT'S GOOD TO BE BACK IN TOWN—BUT IT WOULD BE BETTER IF WE HAD MORE MONEY!

PERHAPS WE'LL ROB SOME—*OH!*

DO MY EYES DECEIVE ME . . . A LIVE PUPPET . . . WITH NO STRINGS?!

WE'VE SOLVED OUR MONEY PROBLEM, GIDDY! STROMBOLI THE PUPPET MASTER WILL PAY US A FORTUNE FOR THAT THING!

STROMBOLI

THE TWO TRICKSTERS WASTED NO TIME IN INTRODUCING THEMSELVES TO THE PUPPET.

AND WHAT'S *YOUR* NAME, CHILD?

PINOCCHIO! I'M OFF TO SCHOOL SO FATHER WILL BE PROUD!

BUT OF COURSE YOU ARE. AND YOU KNOW WHAT WOULD MAKE HIM PROUDEST OF ALL, DON'T YOU?

IF YOU WERE ON *STAGE*!

REALLY?

TRUST ME. SHALL WE GO?

PINOCCHIO *DID* WANT HIS FATHER TO BE PROUD OF HIM, SO OFF HE WENT WITH HONEST JOHN AND GIDEON.

JIMINY TRIED TO CONVINCE PINOCCHIO THAT HONEST JOHN AND GIDEON WERE BAD NEWS, BUT PINOCCHIO WOULDN'T LISTEN!

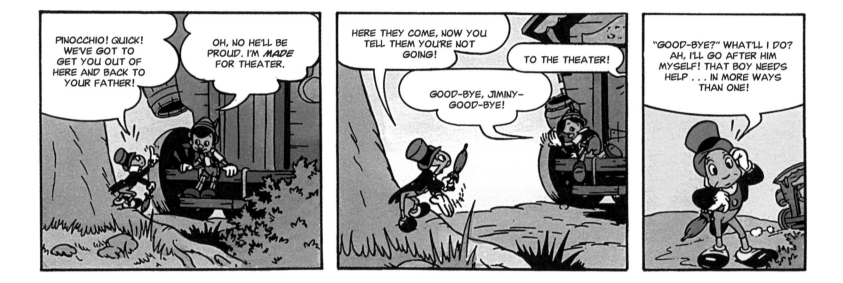

PINOCCHIO! QUICK! WE'VE GOT TO GET YOU OUT OF HERE AND BACK TO YOUR FATHER!

OH, NO HE'LL BE PROUD. I'M *MADE* FOR THEATER.

HERE THEY COME, NOW YOU TELL THEM YOU'RE NOT GOING!

GOOD-BYE, JIMINY— GOOD-BYE!

TO THE THEATER!

"GOOD-BYE?" WHAT'LL I DO? AH, I'LL GO AFTER HIM MYSELF! THAT BOY NEEDS HELP . . . IN MORE WAYS THAN ONE!

SOON PINOCCHIO WAS BEING INTRODUCED TO AN AUDIENCE BY THE PUPPET MASTER, STROMBOLI!

LADIES AND GENTLEMEN, THE GREAT STROMBOLI HAS THE HONOR TO PRESENT THE AMAZING . . .

. . . PINOCCHIO, THE PUPPET WITHOUT STRINGS!

THAT'S ME!

OOPS!

IT WAS JUST ABOUT THE WORST ACT JIMINY HAD EVER SEEN. AND STROMBOLI SEEMED TO AGREE.

THEN, PINOCCHIO LAUNCHED INTO A SONG AND DANCE. HE SEEMED TO REALLY HAVE THE HANG OF IT NOW. STOMBOLI WAS PLEASED. THE CROWD CHEERED!

BUT BACK AT HOME, PINOCCHIO'S DEAR OLD DAD WAS WORRIED SICK ABOUT HIM.

WHERE CAN PINOCCHIO BE? HE SHOULD HAVE BEEN HOME HOURS AGO!

I'M SO WORRIED. HE MUST HAVE GOTTEN LOST—I HAVE TO FIND HIM!

SLAM!

AS THE RAIN POURED DOWN ON THE STREET OUTSIDE, PINOCCHIO WAS SAFE IN STROMBOLI'S CARRIAGE. AT LEAST HE *THOUGHT* HE WAS SAFE!

MY BOY, YOU WERE *SENSATIONAL*!

REALLY?

YES! YOU HAVE A GREAT TALENT FOR THEATER!

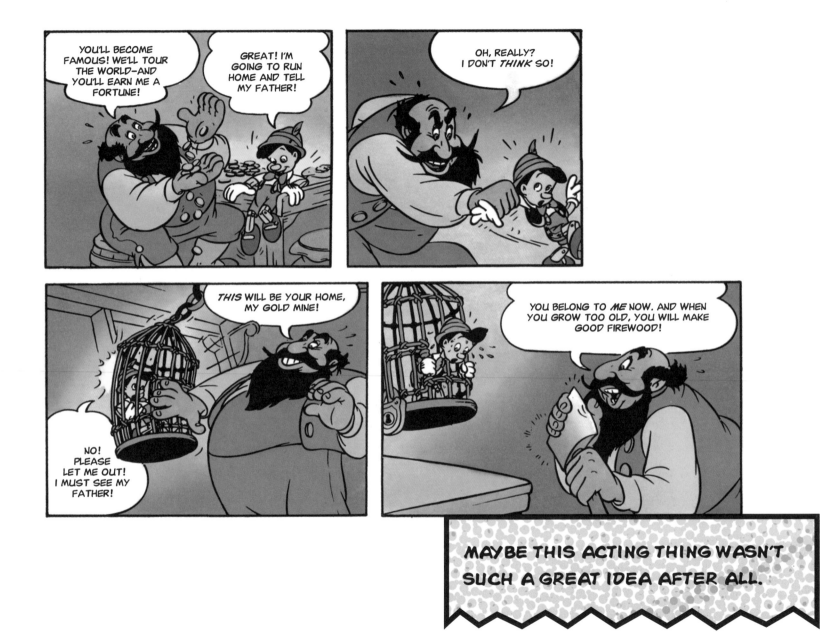

MEANWHILE, JIMINY DECIDED THAT WITH PINOCCHIO'S NEWFOUND FAME, HIS FRIEND PROBABLY WOULDN'T NEED A CONSCIENCE ANYMORE. HE DECIDED TO VISIT HIM INSIDE STROMBOLI'S CARRIAGE TO SAY GOOD-BYE.

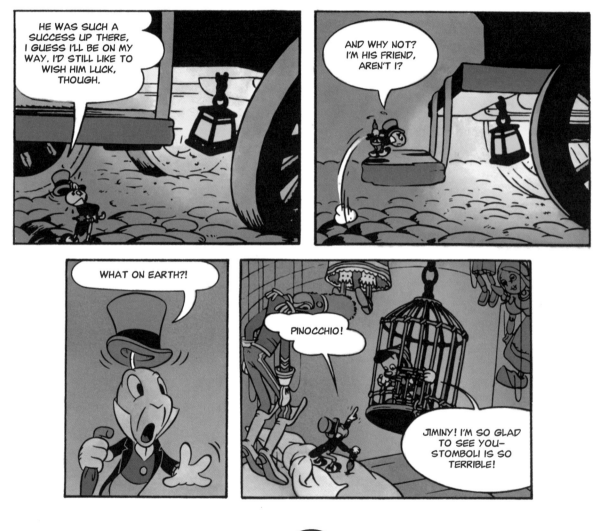

JIMINY WAS HORRIFIED. HE GOT TO WORK RIGHT AWAY TO SAVE HIS FRIEND.

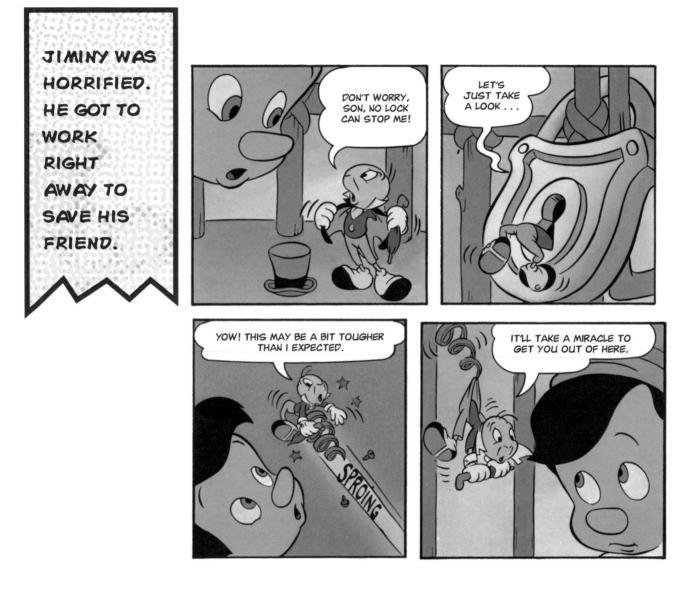

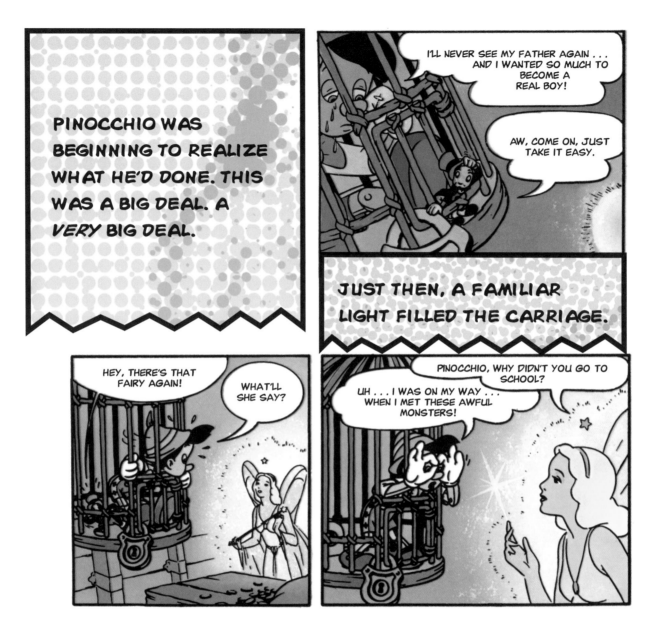

PINOCCHIO WAS BEGINNING TO REALIZE WHAT HE'D DONE. THIS WAS A BIG DEAL. A *VERY* BIG DEAL.

I'LL NEVER SEE MY FATHER AGAIN . . . AND I WANTED SO MUCH TO BECOME A REAL BOY!

AW, COME ON, JUST TAKE IT EASY.

JUST THEN, A FAMILIAR LIGHT FILLED THE CARRIAGE.

HEY, THERE'S THAT FAIRY AGAIN!

WHAT'LL SHE SAY?

PINOCCHIO, WHY DIDN'T YOU GO TO SCHOOL?

UH . . . I WAS ON MY WAY . . . WHEN I MET THESE AWFUL MONSTERS!

PINOCCHIO WAS SO HAPPY TO BE FREE. AND HE WAS SUDDENLY READY TO TURN OVER A NEW LEAF! THEN HE AND JIMINY RACED HOME TO GEPPETTO.

MEANWHILE, BACK IN TOWN, THE TWO CROOKS WHO HAD SOLD PINOCCHIO TO STROMBOLI WERE SITTING INSIDE A DARK AND GLOOMY INN.

WELL, THAT'S WHAT I CALL A GREAT BUSINESS DEAL AND A FINE DAY! WOULDN'T YOU SAY, GIDDY?

WHAT MAKES IT EVEN BETTER IS THAT THE PUPPET STILL THINKS WE'RE HIS FRIENDS!

WHEN BIG MOUTHS TALK, PEOPLE CAN'T HELP BUT LISTEN. AND SOMEONE AT THE NEXT TABLE OVERHEARD THE TWO RASCALS.

EXCUSE ME, FRIENDS— MAY I MAKE YOU AN OFFER?

WE'RE ALWAYS READY TO LISTEN—WHAT HAVE YOU GOT TO SAY?

HOW WOULD YOU FELLAS LIKE TO MAKE A LOT OF MONEY?

AND I DO MEAN A *LOT.*

WHOA . . .

I COLLECT DISOBEDIENT BOYS, AND I TAKE 'EM TO PLEASURE ISLAND. I THINK YOU CAN HELP ME.

HONEST JOHN AND GIDEON HAD NEVER SEEN SO MUCH MONEY!

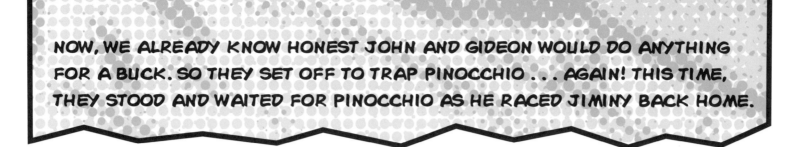

NOW, WE ALREADY KNOW HONEST JOHN AND GIDEON WOULD DO ANYTHING FOR A BUCK. SO THEY SET OFF TO TRAP PINOCCHIO . . . AGAIN! THIS TIME, THEY STOOD AND WAITED FOR PINOCCHIO AS HE RACED JIMINY BACK HOME.

JIMINY'S . . . RUNNING . . . TOO FAST . . . I CAN'T . . . KEEP . . . UP . . .

THERE HE IS AGAIN, THE LITTLE FOOL! NOW HE'S OURS!

OH! HELLO!

PINOCCHIO, SO NICE TO SEE YOU AGAIN. WHAT'S YOUR RUSH?

PINOCCHIO TOLD HONEST JOHN HOW TERRIBLE STROMBOLI WAS, AND THAT HE DIDN'T WANT TO BE AN ACTOR ANYMORE! HE JUST WANTED TO GO HOME TO HIS FATHER.

BUT YOU LOOK SO TIRED—YOU MUST BE ILL.

NO, I WAS JUST HAVING A RACE WITH JIMINY.

HMM . . . I THINK WE'LL HAVE TO EXAMINE THIS YOUNG MAN, DON'T YOU?

OH, DEAR! HIS CHEST SOUNDS TERRIBLE!

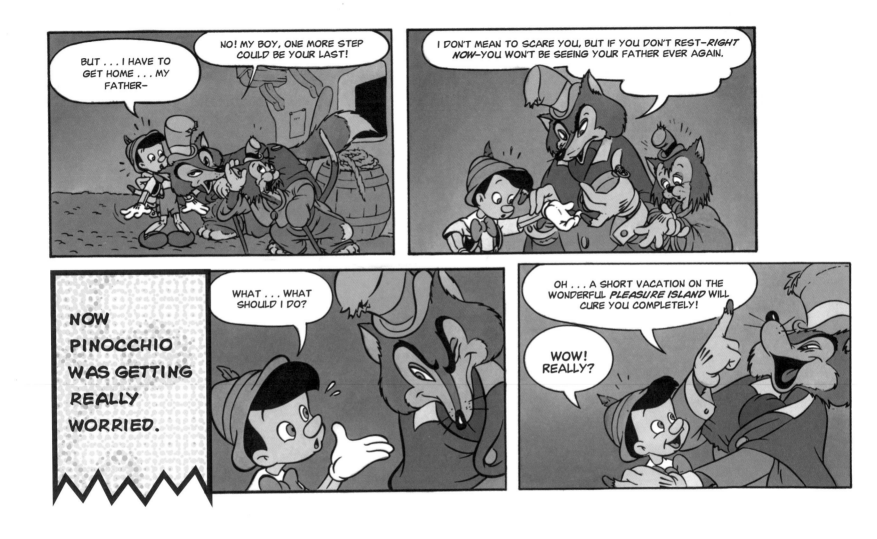

"PLEASURE ISLAND." PINOCCHIO LIKED THE SOUND OF THAT. HE WAS FEELING BETTER ALREADY.

OH, YES. IT'S A CHILDREN'S PARADISE— CANDY GROWS ON TREES. AND YOU CAN DO WHATEVER YOU WANT TO!

BUT—I—I CAN'T GO.

WHY, OF COURSE YOU CAN. I'M GIVING YOU MY TICKET.

AND SO THE TWO BAD GUYS TOOK OFF WITH THE TRUSTING YOUNG PUPPET.

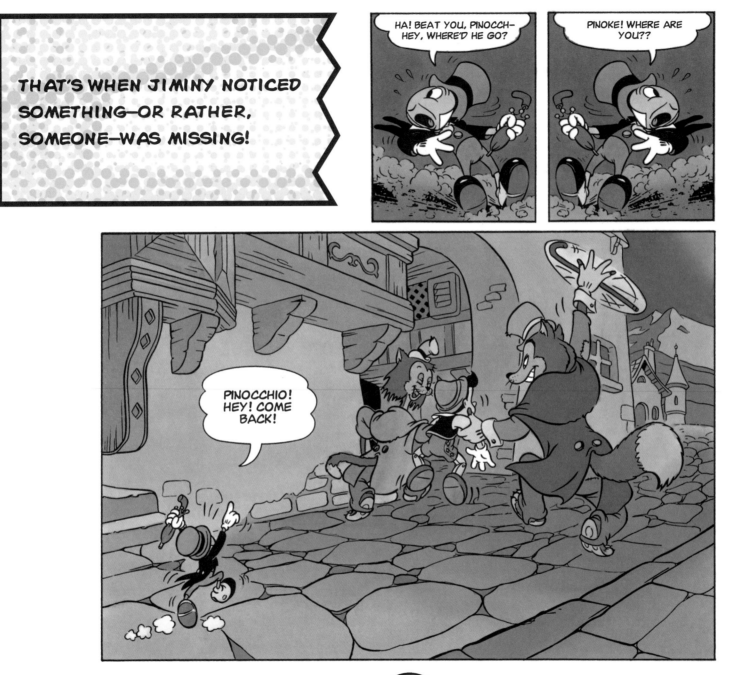

THAT'S WHEN JIMINY NOTICED SOMETHING—OR RATHER, SOMEONE—WAS MISSING!

HA! BEAT YOU, PINOCCH— HEY, WHERE'D HE GO?

PINOKE! WHERE ARE YOU??

PINOCCHIO! HEY! COME BACK!

PINOCCHIO SOON FOUND HIMSELF ON A BIG OL' WAGON, HEADING TO A FAR-OFF ISLAND!

ON BOARD, PINOCCHIO MET A BOY NAMED LAMPWICK, WHO SEEMED PRETTY EXCITED ABOUT HIS TRIP TO PLEASURE ISLAND, TOO.

I'VE NEVER BEEN TO PLEASURE ISLAND.

ME NEITHER—THEY SAY IT'S SWELL THOUGH!

THE COACH-MAN STOPPED THE WAGON NEAR A DOCKED BOAT.

ALL ABOARD, KIDS!

AND IT WASN'T LONG BEFORE THAT BOAT BROUGHT PINOCCHIO, LAMPWICK, AND THE REST OF THE KIDS RIGHT TO PLEASURE ISLAND!

YAY! PLEASURE ISLAND!

HOORAY!

ARE CANDY AND ICE CREAM REALLY FREE HERE?

SURE—AND THAT'S NOT ALL. EVERYTHING YOU CAN'T *NORMALLY* DO IS *FINE* HERE!

IT'S JUST LIKE THEY SAID!

ISN'T IT SWELL? THE CIRCUS, FIREWORKS—ONE BIG PARTY!

THERE WERE NO RULES ON PLEASURE ISLAND. AND LAMPWICK WANTED TO PROVE THAT TO PINOCCHIO.

I . . . I DON'T KNOW ABOUT THAT.

BUT IT'S FUN!

AND THERE'S NOBODY HERE TO STOP YOU!

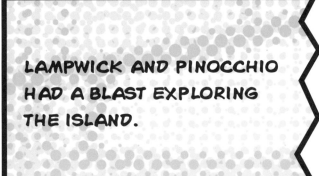

LAMPWICK AND PINOCCHIO HAD A BLAST EXPLORING THE ISLAND.

CHERRY PIES AND CANDY BARS ON THE SAME TREE? WOW!

AND YOU CAN HELP YOURSELF TO THAT MOUNTAIN—IT'S MADE OF ICE CREAM!

AND A LEMONADE FOUNTAIN!

AIN'T IT GREAT? AND THIS IS ONLY THE BEGINNING!

ALL THE KIDS WERE SO OVERJOYED AT THEIR NEWFOUND FREEDOM THAT THEY DIDN'T PAY ANY ATTENTION TO THE DRIVER WHO'D BROUGHT THEM TO THE ISLAND . . . AND THAT WAS JUST WHAT THE EVIL COACHMAN HAD INTENDED . . .

NOW . . . TO TRAP THESE LITTLE SCOUNDRELS . . .

SHUT THE DOORS AND LOCK THEM TIGHT!

THE COACHMAN MOTIONED TO A MYSTERIOUS DOORWAY, AND HIS GOONS CLOSED AND LOCKED THE DOORS AS HE HAD DEMANDED. WHAT COULD BE GOING ON IN THERE?

THE HOURS PASSED, AND THE PLEASURE ISLAND CARNIVAL WAS IN RUINS. THE KIDS HAD REALLY DONE A NUMBER ON IT.

AND JIMINY WAS LOOKING FOR HIS FRIEND!

THIS PLACE IS BIG—I HOPE I CAN FIND PINOCCHIO!

PINOCCHIO! WHERE *ARE* YOU?

IN FACT, THE WAYWARD LITTLE PUPPET WAS QUITE CLOSE. BUT HE COULDN'T—OR DIDN'T WANT TO—HEAR HIS CONSCIENC

PINOCCHIO HAD A FEELING THIS WHOLE SMOKING THING WASN'T SUCH A GOOD IDEA. BUT HE WANTED TO BE COOL, LIKE LAMPWICK.

ONE PUFF, HOWEVER, CONVINCED HIM THAT MAYBE LAMPWICK'S SMOKING WASN'T SO COOL AFTER ALL.

OKAY, KID! YOUR SHOT!

UM . . . SURE . . . IF I CAN FIND THE BALL . . .

JIMINY HAD
HAD IT!

THAT'S IT! I'M THROUGH WITH YOU!

BUT AS JIMINY LEFT,
HE PASSED THE DOOR
THAT THE COACHMAN
HAD CLOSED EARLIER.
HE PEEKED IN AND
SAW SOMETHING
COMPLETELY AWFUL!

OH . . . OH NO! NO!

JIMINY COULD HARDLY BELIEVE HIS EYES! THE BOYS WHO HAD BEEN BROUGHT TO THE ISLAND HAD BEEN TURNED INTO DONKEYS!

YOU BOYS HAVE HAD YOUR FUN, NOW PAY FOR IT!

REMEMBER, YOU'RE DONKEYS NOW, AND YOU'LL WORK LIKE DONKEYS!

I HAVE TO WARN PINOCCHIO!

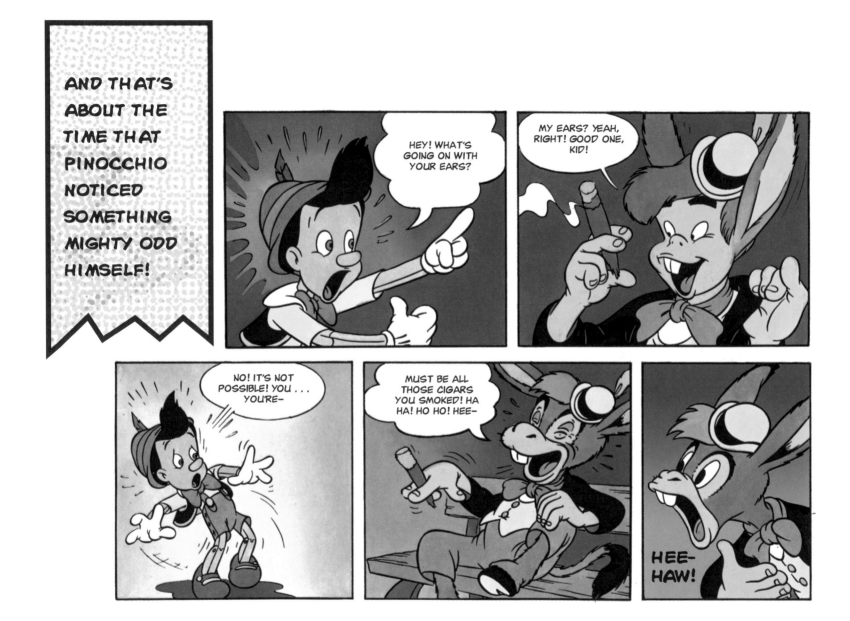

THAT'S THE WAY IT ALWAYS IS, IT SEEMS . . .

... YOU NEVER HEAR YOUR CONSCIENCE UNTIL IT'S TOO LATE! AND THAT'S JUST WHEN JIMINY CAUGHT UP WITH PINOCCHIO.

JIMINY! WHAT'S HAPPENING TO ME?

COME ON, QUICK! BEFORE YOU GET ANY WORSE!

THAT'S WHAT THOSE CROOKS ARE UP TO! THEY TEMPT LAZY, BAD BOYS, AND ONCE THEY'RE HERE—

—THEY TURN THEM INTO DONKEYS AND MAKE THEM SLAVES! LET'S GO!

JIMINY AND PINOCCHIO WERE SO SCARED THAT THEY SWAM ALL THE WAY HOME. BOY, WERE THEY GLAD TO BE BACK! BUT WHEN THEY GOT THERE, PINOCCHIO DIDN'T EXACTLY RECEIVE THE WARM WELCOME HE'D EXPECTED.

FATHER! FATHER! IT'S ME! I'M HOME!

HE'S . . . HE'S GONE.

HE MUST HAVE LEFT BECAUSE I LET HIM DOWN.

JUST THEN, A DOVE APPEARED IN THE SAME MYSTERIOUS WAY THE BLUE FAIRY HAD! AND IT WAS CARRYING SOMETHING!

IT WAS A LETTER ABOUT GEPPETTO.

THE LETTER SAID THAT GEPPETTO WENT LOOKING FOR HIS SON AND WAS NOW TRAPPED INSIDE A WHALE NAMED MONSTRO! EVEN THOUGH IT WOULD BE DANGEROUS, PINOCCHIO KNEW WHAT HE HAD TO DO! HE TIED A ROCK AROUND HIS TAIL TO HELP HIM SINK AND JUMPED!

THE FRIENDS DIDN'T KNOW IT, BUT NOT FAR AWAY, MONSTRO WAS PRETENDING TO SLEEP SO HE COULD TRICK A SCHOOL OF TUNA AND HAVE THEM FOR DINNER!

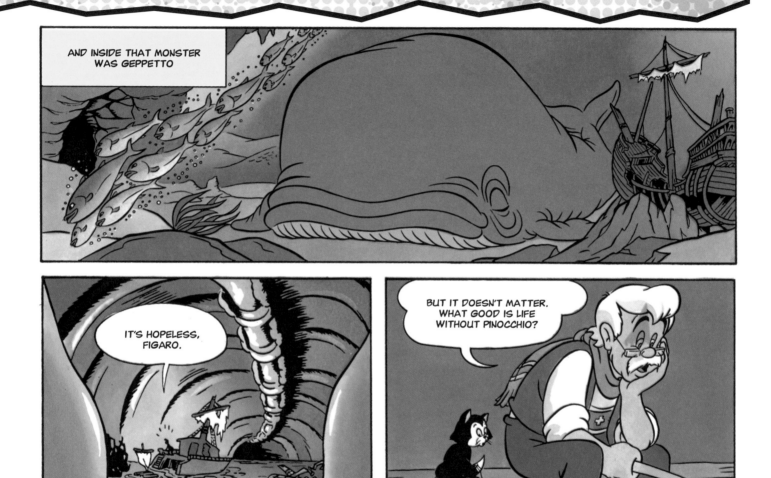

AND INSIDE THAT MONSTER WAS GEPPETTO

IT'S HOPELESS, FIGARO.

BUT IT DOESN'T MATTER. WHAT GOOD IS LIFE WITHOUT PINOCCHIO?

PINOCCHIO HAD GOTTEN CAUGHT UP WITH THE FISH AND WOUND UP IN THE WHALE'S BELLY, TOO!

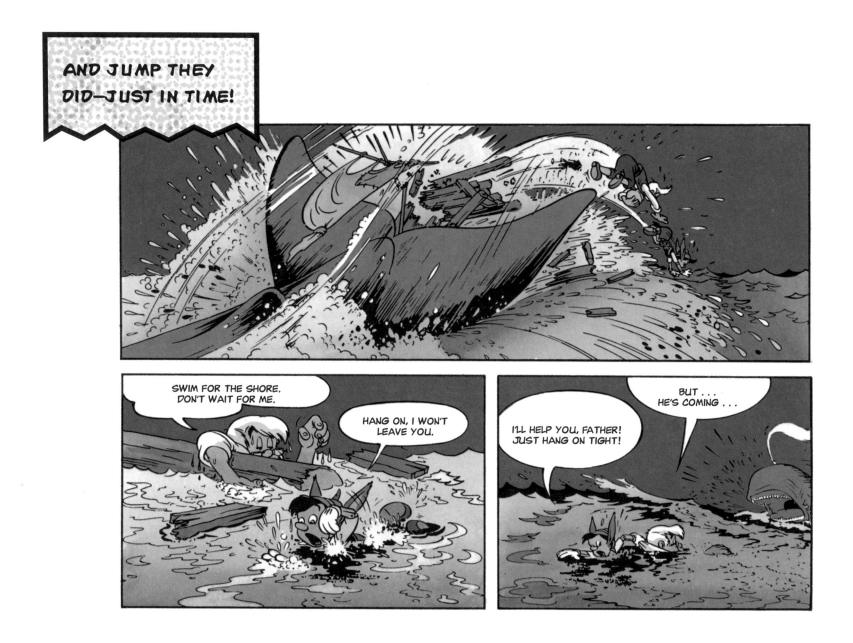

MONSTRO MISSED THEM—BUT JUST BARELY! THEY WERE TOSSED AROUND LIKE SCRAPS OF PAPER IN A HURRICANE! THEY EVENTUALLY WASHED ASHORE . . .

GEPPETTO CARRIED PINOCCHIO BACK HOME. HE KNELT BY HIS SON'S BEDSIDE AND CRIED. PINOCCHIO HAD SAVED HIM... AT THE HIGHEST PRICE.

BUT THE BLUE FAIRY HAD PROMISED PINOCCHIO THAT IF HE PROVED TO BE BRAVE, TRUTHFUL, AND UNSELFISH, HE WOULD BE A REAL BOY. AND SHE WAS KEEPING HER WORD!

AWAKE, PINOCCHIO, AWAKE!

GEE!

FATHER! I'M *ALIVE*! AND I'M A *REAL BOY* NOW!

YOU'RE *ALIVE*! AND A *REAL BOY*!

THIS IS A STORY OF HOPE AND RENEWAL. OF DARKEST DAYS . . .

. . . AND THE HAPPIEST OF TIMES . . .

IN NO TIME FLAT, BAMBI HAD LEARNED HOW TO WALK. AND HIS MOM SHOWED HIM THE FOREST.

THERE WERE SO MANY GREAT THINGS TO SEE—AND EVERY ONE OF THEM WAS NEW TO BAMBI.

TIME PASSED, AND SOON BAMBI WAS AN EXPERT AT ALL THAT WALKING AND TALKING STUFF. HIS MOTHER DECIDED IT WAS TIME TO SHOW HIM SOME OF THE WORLD *BEYOND* THE EDGE OF THE FOREST.

TODAY, I'M GOING TO TAKE YOU TO THE MEADOW.

WHAT'S THE MEADOW, MOTHER?

THIS IS.

BAMBI HAD NEVER SEEN ANYTHING LIKE IT! HE JUMPED RIGHT IN!

OH, IT'S SO BEAUTIFUL, MOTHER! I—

BAMBI! NO!

YOU MUST *NEVER* RUSH OUT ON THE MEADOW!

THE MEADOW IS BEAUTIFUL, BUT IT'S VERY *DANGEROUS*, TOO. WE MUST ALWAYS BE CAREFUL.

MEANWHILE, BAMBI WANDERED OFF TO EXPLORE THE REST OF THE MEADOW. HE STOPPED AT A STREAM, AND THERE . . .

GOOD MORNING.

BAMBI HAD SEEN LOTS OF ANIMALS, BUT BESIDES HIS MOTHER, HE'D NEVER SEEN A FAWN.

. . . SO HE RAN!

AN ENORMOUS HERD OF DEER BURST OUT OF THE FOREST!

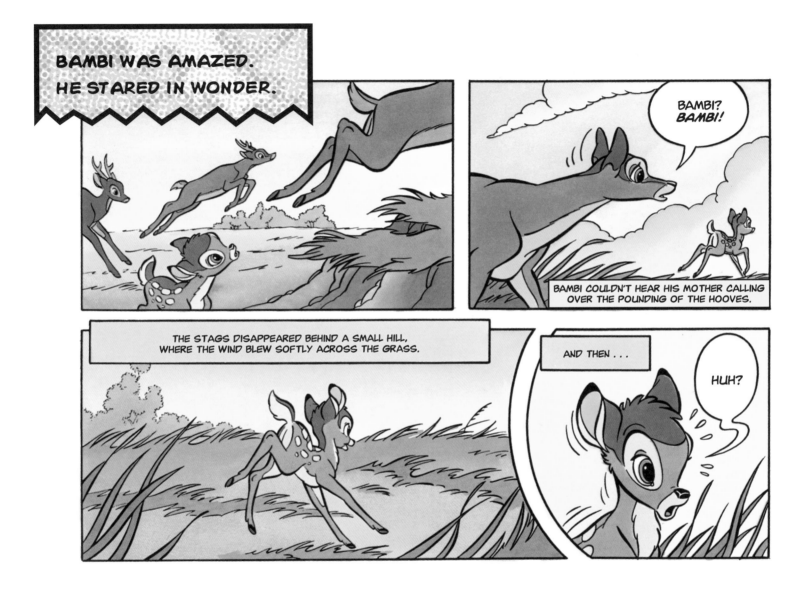

AS SOON AS HE COULD, BAMBI RUSHED BACK TO SAFETY.

BAMBI'S MOM WAS PRETTY MAD!

BAMBI, YOU MUST BE MORE CAREFUL—YOU'RE TOO YOUNG TO BE WITH THOSE GROWN-UPS!

I WON'T DO IT AGAIN, MOTHER—I PROMISE.

THEN, SOMETHING ELSE CAUGHT BAMBI'S MOM'S ATTENTION. BAMBI TURNED SO HE, TOO, COULD SEE WHAT SHE WAS LOOKING AT.

IT WAS THE LARGEST, MOST AMAZING ANIMAL BAMBI HAD EVER SEEN.

NO ONE EVEN BREATHED AS THE MIGHTY BUCK WALKED BY.

SUDDENLY, STARTLED, THE GREAT PRINCE LEAPED UP AND RAN. AS SOON AS HE DID, EVERYONE ELSE FOLLOWED. BAMBI COULDN'T FIND HIS MOM IN ALL THE CONFUSION!

MOTHER! WHERE ARE YOU?

AND THEN, THE GREAT PRINCE RETURNED. HE TOLD BAMBI TO FOLLOW HIM, AND BAMBI DIDN'T HAVE TO THINK TWICE!

THE GREAT PRINCE DROPPED BAMBI OFF WITH HIS MOTHER IN A SAFE PART OF THE FOREST, AND THEN RAN OFF IN ANOTHER DIRECTION.

BANG! BANG!

A BUNCH OF LOUD NOISES SOUNDED. BAMBI HAD NEVER HEARD ANYTHING LIKE IT BEFORE! THEN HIS MOTHER EXPLAINED . . .

MAN WAS IN THE FOREST . . .

TIME PASSED AND THE LEAVES OF THE FOREST BEGAN TO CHANGE COLOR.

THIS IS AUTUMN, WHEN NATURE PREPARES FOR ITS LONG WINTER SLEEP. SOON EVERYTHING WILL BE DIFFERENT—YOU'LL GROW A WINTER COAT, FOR THE WEATHER WILL BE VERY COLD.

SOME ANIMALS FOUND PLACES UNDERGROUND, WHERE THEY COULD SLEEP UNTIL SPRING—AND SOME, LIKE FRIEND OWL, JUST SNUGGLED UP IN THEIR HOMES!

BAMBI REALLY LIKED THE FALL. BUT SOON, AUTUMN, LIKE SPRING AND SUMMER BEFORE, CAME TO AN END . . .

...AND ONE MORNING, BAMBI WOKE UP AND FOUND THE FOREST COVERED IN WHITE! WINTER HAD ARRIVED!

HMM?

HMM!

SPLOSH!

THUMPER SHOWED BAMBI HOW TO
WALK ON THE SNOW, AND THEY
RAN TO THE ICED-OVER POND!

BAMBI THOUGHT THAT SLIDING ON THE ICE LOOKED LIKE A LOT OF FUN.
BUT IT ALSO LOOKED TRICKY!

THE WEATHER CONTINUED TO GET COLDER, AND IT SNOWED ALL WINTER! DURING THE COLD SEASON, THERE WAS LITTLE TO EAT.

I'M SO HUNGRY, MOTHER.

I KNOW, BAMBI. IT'LL BE SPRING SOON, AND WE'LL FIND FOOD THEN.

AND THEN, THE WINTER FINALLY STARTED TO THAW. THERE WAS A LITTLE BIT OF NEW SPRING GRASS SPROUTING, AND BAMBI AND HIS MOM WERE HAPPY TO BE EATING AGAIN! BUT SUDDENLY, BAMBI'S MOTHER STARTED, THE SAME WAY THE GREAT PRINCE HAD WHEN MAN WAS IN THE FOREST!

THE WORLD CONTINUED TO TURN. THE SNOW MELTED. AND SOON IT WAS SPRING AGAIN.

NOT ONLY WERE THE FLOWERS AND PLANTS GROWING. BUT SOME OLD FRIENDS WERE, TOO!

IT SEEMED LIKE EVERYONE WAS OUT AND ABOUT.

THE FRIENDS WERE SO HAPPY TO BE TOGETHER AGAIN. BUT FRIEND OWL, PARTY POOPER THAT HE WAS, WARNED THEM ABOUT THE GREAT DANGER OF SPRINGTIME. SPRING COULD MAKE THEM FALL IN LOVE! AND THAT COULD MAKE THEM LOSE THEIR MINDS! BUT THE FRIENDS WERE CONFIDENT THAT THEY WOULDN'T FALL INTO THAT TRAP.

BUT BAMBI WASN'T THE ONLY ONE INTERESTED IN FALINE. ANOTHER STAG APPEARED, READY TO FIGHT FOR HER! THE STAG STARTED TO BOTHER FALINE. AND BAMBI WASN'T ABOUT TO LET HIM GET AWAY WITH THAT.

BAMBI AND THE STAG BASHED INTO EACH OTHER. THE TWO DEER FOUGHT LIKE WILD.

THE OTHER DEER WAS OLDER AND STRONGER. BUT BAMBI DEFEATED HIS RIVAL!

THERE WAS NOTHING THAT BAMBI WANTED MORE THAN TO BE WITH FALINE ALL THE TIME.

THINGS SEEMED PERFECT.

BUT ONE MORNING, AS BAMBI WALKED THROUGH THE FOREST,
HE NOTICED SOMETHING DIFFERENT—HOUSES . . . AND SMOKE!
THEN HIS FATHER, THE GREAT PRINCE, APPEARED, AND EXPLAINED.

IT'S MAN.
HE'S HERE AGAIN.

BUT BAMBI WASN'T GOING TO LEAVE WITHOUT FALINE! HE SEARCHED EVERYWHERE FOR HER. AND WHEN HE FINALLY FOUND HER, SHE WAS IN DEEP, DEEP TROUBLE! MAN'S DOGS HAD SURROUNDED HER! BUT SHE WOULDN'T BE IN A BIND FOR LONG. NOT IF BAMBI COULD HELP IT!

FALINE ESCAPED WITH BAMBI'S HELP. BUT NOW BAMBI HAD ONLY ONE WAY OUT—UP THE MOUNTAINSIDE! HE SCRAMBLED FOR SAFETY, SENDING ROCKS CRASHING DOWN ON THE DOGS.

AT THE TOP, HE CAME TO THE EDGE OF A HUGE CREVICE. WITH A GREAT LEAP, HE JUMPED TO THE OTHER SIDE. BUT AS HE LANDED . . .

. . . HE WAS HIT WITH A BULLET, AND COLLAPSED IN PAIN!

MEANWHILE, BACK AT THE HUNTERS' CAMP, AN UNATTENDED FIRE GREW OUT OF CONTROL. THE WHOLE FOREST FILLED WITH FLAMES AND SMOKE!

THE FLAMES GREW CLOSER
AND CLOSER TO BAMBI.

THEN, THE GREAT PRINCE,
APPEARED AGAIN!

WE MUST KEEP GOING OR—

LOOK OUT!

A FLAMING TREE CRASHED DOWN RIGHT IN FRONT OF THE TWO DEER!

CRRAAAACCCK!

WITH NO OTHER WAY OUT, THE TRAPPED DEER HAD NO CHOICE BUT TO LEAP DOWN THE FOREST'S MASSIVE WATERFALL!

THE OTHER BANK WAS
SAFE FROM THE
FLAMES. AND FALINE
WAS WAITING THERE FOR
BAMBI AND HIS FATHER!

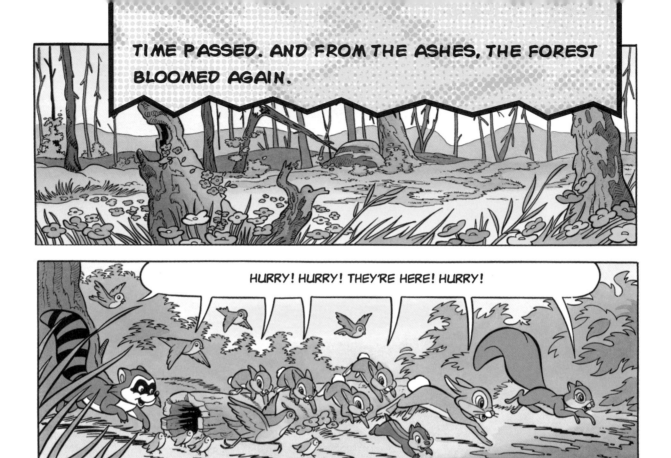

THE ANIMALS TURNED TO SEE THE GREAT PRINCE AND HIS SON, BAMBI, ANOTHER GREAT PRINCE, LOOKING DOWN OVER THE FOREST.

WITH TRUST AND CONFIDENCE IN HIS SON, THE GREAT PRINCE NODDED, AND WALKED AWAY INTO THE FOREST.

AND BAM

HIS FRIE

HE HAD

MADE HI

WOULD